THE WAY BACK

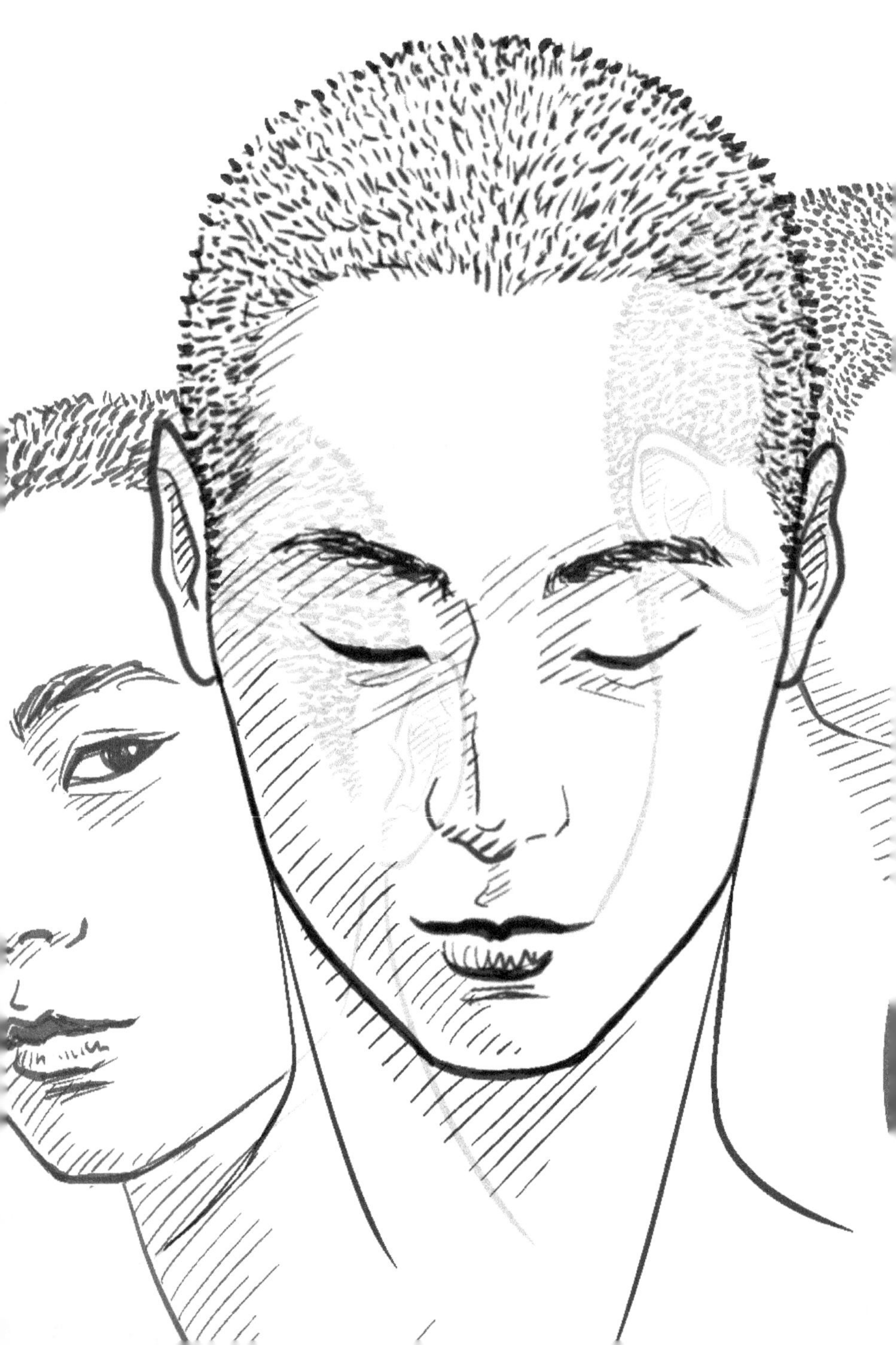

THE WAY BACK

Edward Gunawan

Book and Cover Design: Miah Jeffra and Jason Lipeles
Cover Image by Elbert Lim
Courtesy of the artist
Copyright © 2022 Edward Gunawan
ISBN:

Cataloging-in-publication data is available from the Library of Congress

This book has been made possible, in part, by a grant from the Whiting Foundation

Printed in the United States of America

Foglifter Press
San Francisco, California
www.foglifterpress.com

To Amah —

for
whispering
over my shoulders
these directions
that led me
back home

TABLE OF CONTENTS

The Question Next Time

At the consulate to renew my passport, I arrive an hour early. Un-opened book by my side, feet tapping. I stare at the forms in my hands.

I'd filled out the details of my particulars: Name, sex, occupation. Married? Check. Emergency contact? Jake. Stopping at: Relationship. I haven't declared in any official capacity in my home country.

I haven't had to. Until now.

No Spouse in my native tongue to hide behind. Called into a room where a scowling man collects my face and fingerprints, I sit and wait.

And wait.

To unleash with full force of indignance the counter-arguments I'd rehearsed. *No, I'm not the Wife!* And *Yes, I'm Husband to a man.*

But the questions never come. I'll be ready next time.

Love Refugees

We   who broke our names to fit the contours and curls of their mouths; who spoke our mother tongues with shame and celebrated our New Year in secret.

We   who rolled our windows up and shut the doors double-barred; who kept them out by locking ourselves in.

We   who are spared of our dignity when it's never theirs to give; who belong to no nation where freedom has never been free.

We are panhandlers really. Begging for the loose change of democracy. Philosophers practicing the religious art of grateful resiliency.

Yes, we'll take what we can get, what we're given — any alm, any scrap, any crumb.

Thank you, sir, for your generosity. Yes, it's more than enough, sir. It's our own damn fault anyway. What can we say, it's our fate as

love refugees.

tap tap tap

creaking open, footsteps approach. stream hisses at the porcelain. a gurgling flush and the door slams shut.

tap tap tap

another creak. jeans rustling, heavy feet shuffling. sticky shoe squeaks through the partition, and it too goes —

tap tap tap

metallic clang. roll unspooling. held breath and a swallowed gulp: *shhhhh, no one has to know...*

tap tap tap

a tentative yes, a guttural moan, syncopated whispers of hungry beasts, sharp teeth bright and blinding in the damp and dark.

tap tap tap

fireworks exploding. flurries of zipping, flushing, footsteps fading, closed door echoing — a wave of silence frozen in mid-air.

The Man on the Train

We were two men taking drags off our cigarettes, blowing smoke to mask the bathroom stench behind us — doors open, reeking of days-old piss. We had just covered the basics: *Where are you coming from?* Marrakech. *Where are you going?* Fez. *Same, me too.*

Cocking his neck, he then asked: *Traveling alone?*

*

After criss-crossing Morocco for the past week, I was on the second leg of my day-long train journey, sharing the carriage with five other passengers, seated three along each row. I was in the middle seat. To the right, by the window of rolling green hills, a teenage couple sat across each other, giddily giggling at their phone screens. On my left, a young father with fashionably-trimmed stubble fussed over his headscarf-wrapped wife and their cooing toddler, sitting directly opposite to us. While her husband grunted a few yes and nos in English back to me, she had never once looked me in the eye. The air outside was mid-fall cool, but inside the enclosed quarter of the carriage, heat from the floor vent draped its stifling coat over us.

Roaming along the length of the train, I squeezed by carts of piping-hot empana-da-like pastries and wild-hair musicians strumming their guitars before finally finding my way to the dining carriage for coffee and chips. I thought of returning to my book. But head spinning, as though drowning in an ocean of words, rocking and rollicking in the waves with each rumbling jerky motion of the creaking vehicle, I parked myself instead in between two carriages — the makeshift smoking corner I had stumbled upon.

The green blurs sped by.

I had just lit my first cigarette when a short stocky man in a faded brown leather jacket approached. He asked for a spare and I obliged. Curly graying hair bouncing over his gold-rimmed reading glasses, he could have been a philosophy professor if I had met him in another place or time.

When he ever-casually posed the loaded question at me, I kept my guard up. Headlines of "Solo Traveler Robbed on a Train" or "Tourist Kidnapped While Smoking" tore through my brain in those milliseconds. All the same, I nodded in affirmation.

He continued on: *No kids?* No. *Wife?* I shook my head. *How about girlfriend?* he pressed further, a gleeful grin flashing across his face now. When I again muttered no, he broke into a fit of belly-laughs as though we were two middle-aged men bonding at a dinner party after our wives had discarded us in the corner. How lucky and free you must be, he seemed to telegraph, so unencumbered by all these wordly responsibilities.

I took another puff, before lobbing the same questions back at him. *No, no kids... Never been married either...* And what do you do in Fez? *Business.* What kind? *Oh, a spa.* Like a massage spa? *Yes, yes. You like massage?* Of course. I mean, who doesn't? Without missing a beat, he asked: *Would you like one?* My sudden muteness must have conveyed my apprehension as he immediately followed up with: *No, not with me. Of course not.* Then, eyes darting around the empty carriage and voice dropping to a conspiratorial whisper, he clarified himself: *I have boys. You like boys?*

I was right. This had been a pick-up after all.

But even I hadn't expected this turn of events. I widened my stance and smoothed out the wool of my sweater — equally appalled as I was impressed. Had I been so obvious to have given myself away? Did I need to butch it up a little more, especially since I was making my way through some of the smaller towns on this trip?

While Morocco and Indonesia are two very different countries, they share many bone-wearily familiar similarities — the call-to-prayer adzan that blasted through the hotel's windows every dawn; the common greetings of Assalamualaikum and perfunctory Insya Allah and Bismillah peppered into daily conversations; and the indisputable fact that many of us have been cruelly harassed and persecuted, if not jailed, just for being queer. Newspaper reports of George Michael's lewd-act arrest from long-ago flashed across the screen projection of my mind. Was this man in front of me one of those undercover cops? Could this be an entrapment sting?

In response to my polite smile, he thrusted his cell phone into my direct line of vision. *Want to see photos?* I immediately declined with a shrug, as though miming a "You do you, dude. But I'm good." Like a cultural anthropologist on an assignment, I launched into a series of questions: Is the spa only for men? How long have you been running it? Lastly, are you scared? (*Yes, yes,* and he scoffed at the last one).

He must have realized that I was no good for business, for he soon flicked his butt on the floor before snubbing it out with the outsole of his leather shoe. *Thanks for the cigarette again.* Then, he slipped a business card into the front pocket of my shirt before disappearing into the hall and into his carriage.

*

I didn't call him when I got to Fez, as curious as I was. The boys he alluded to never stopped haunting my imagination, long after the train ride. Were they olive-skinned

Adonises with come-hither long lashes and open-chest tight shirts displaying their bulging muscles and unabashed virility? Or were they more emaciated frail twinks in ankle-chain bondage, never seeing the light of day in some basement dungeon?

The sex-positive West Coast liberal in me chided these neo-colonialist assumptions. Why couldn't they also be proudly empowered men who took on the work they could find for themselves, making the money they needed to support themselves and their families? After all, for many folks in many different parts of the world, this is still how we connect with one another, seeking comfort in simple carnal pleasures.

Most of all, I wanted to ask: Why had he taken the risk in propositioning me in broad daylight and in public? Was it due to the fact I was traveling on my own, conspicuously yellow in the sea of dark-featured Moroccan faces? How could he have known that I wouldn't report him to the authorities?

For the next few days, I took his card out during my smoke break — fingering the blunt corner edges that scraped against the center flesh of my palm. Yes, the encounter happened, I reminded myself.

The card is real. And so are we.

Dear Future Ex

One night you will bump into me on a crowded dance floor. Cobwebs of laser lights atop the sticky swarm of shirtless men. Eyes rolling to the back of our sockets. Rippling abs glisten amidst the *throb a-throb throb* and the *thump a-thump thump*.

We dance — you, your boyfriend, me, and mine — in a tight circle. Chest to chest. Breath steaming our cheeks. Palms snug in the back pockets of soaking jeans. You lean on me, whispering: *He's a keeper.* I tilt my head, grinning: *So is yours.*

We shuffle out onto the patio, our boyfriends making small talk. Behind us, the door opens and closes — the *throb a-throb throb* and the *thump a-thump thump* drifting in and out. The smoke of our cigarettes.

You look good. I'm glad he makes you happy. Squeezing your thigh, the same one I know so well. Years, in a flash, of running and running, falling and stumbling.

I leave the club shortly with the boyfriend. We will break up in a few months. And you'll break up with yours too. But you stay and you play 'til the lights come up. 'Til the sun rises. 'Til the *throb a-throb throb* and the *thump a-thump thump* and the men, there no longer.

Cognitive Reframing

An homage to "ars pasifika" by Craig Santos Perez

When voices of the world scream too loudly for me to be

S I L E N T

then with a prick of my ears I rearrange the letters to

L I S T E N

Insufferable Joy

If this were a poem

I'd begin with the photograph on our wedding invitation. Taken on a beach on Jake's birthday. Our backs in silhouette, two men, leaning on each other's shoulders, kissing.

If this were a painting

I'd color in that ball of deep red crimson sun, plunging down from the orange sky. Into the bluest ocean, awashed in golden sepia.

If this were a film

I'd zoom in on that digital mock-up, dressed in clean modern fonts, minimalist design. How I had opened and closed and reopened the file on my laptop screen, again and again, over and over, aligning each line, moving the text around 'til I got it just right. Before arriving on the desktop of that specialty printer I found, having called in vain a dozen of them. How the invitation was then printed in small batches. Five to be exact. And I delivered one in person to my mother.

If this were a play

I'd open with the scene in a restaurant. Five months prior to me handing that envelope to her. *I'm proposing*, I said while passing the dishes around. *You're doing it alone*, she asked, *right?* My father raised his eyebrows before changing the conversation. Because lamaran are multi-day communal affairs where I come from, with the bride's family paying a visit to the groom's, armed with baskets of jewelry and cash for dowries. But who is the bride here? And who is going to whose house exactly?

If this were an essay

I'd share a decidedly Indonesian custom. Of guests declining beverages offered by the host on house visits. A minimum of two times. Before finally sipping it. No matter how thirsty we were. Chugging it down would be uncouth.

I'd invited my parents to the wedding more than three times. The first time, I admit I'd done it in the pretext of an auspicious date request. I am my mother's son after all. She caught it immediately and declined.

If this were a short story

I'd set the scene up in my therapist's office. As he asked me again, *Are you inviting them? Or are you asking for permission?* I'd tell him that I'm seeking their blessing, as any child would. *Wouldn't anyone be disappointed if their parents were not present for such a momentous occasion?* And he'd challenge me, *Why does it matter if they came or not?*

I'd then flashback to another session. My first one ever. Two decades prior. She, my mother, was there too. If conversion is what she's looking for, I'm not for you, he muttered under his breath while leading us out of the door. I turned to face him, suddenly noticing the slight swish of his wrist.

If this were a novel

I'd insert the memory of an 11-year-old boy, tearing his portfolio of fashion illustrations, in front of his mother who begged him in tears to do so. He stared at the women in puffy ball gowns from these pages. The drawings he had spent all summer on. They all landed in the trash.

I'd slip in next that I went back to my parents' house the following day. Ours never did make it on the rack of other invitations they received from their friends and our relatives.

If this were a historical tome

I'd write about how I grew up seeing my father locking the front door of our house with two metal bars. Outside, barbed wires sit atop our fences. Every block, in our suburban neighborhood, was makeshift gates and security checkpoints. Looting, arson, rape, massacre. The ghost of 1965 haunting us again in 1998.

If this were a memoir

I'd spend pages on my father's Chinese school getting shuttered overnight. How he never did get to finish high school. Neither did my mother. How they both changed their names on their IDs. How, over the years, we celebrated our New Year, in silence and in the dark. And how he lost his father as a teenager. He, the youngest one out of 12. From two households. His mother was the second wife. My mother too was lost in the shuffle of nine other siblings. Inhospitable households and a callous country. Systematic shame and hand-me-down traumas. A loss, private and public, both micro and macro.

If this were a self-help book

I'd recount the incident as a humorous anecdote. Straddling the line between acceptance and surrender. With enviable vulnerability. Seeing them as they are, I'd tell myself and the readers: *These things are beyond my control. So I let go.* Gallantly substituting I *want* them to come with I *would like* them to come. For in this way, if they decide not to, and they are after all in possession of the free will to make their own decisions, it would still be all right. That *I* would still be all right. I would not expect. But I shall hope. Still. Actually, I shall not use *shall.* Wasn't this one of my therapist's reminders? *Shall is something that won't happen.* What's a broken wish but a torture device?

If this were a writing handbook

I'd convince myself that authors couldn't possibly force the characters in our stories into doing what we wanted for them. They're no supporting figures. But heroes in their own narratives. Who exercise their own agencies, make their own minds, speak their own lines, and take their own course of action. I cannot, must not, impose my plot on them. It's impossible to direct a reenactment of the scenes I've written, no matter how beautiful or pathos.

If this were an opera

I'd take the opportunity to wallow in the aria of my self-pity so loudly. The catharsis for a lifetime's accumulation of Waiting. And Yearning. And Longing. For something that would never come. I never did learn my lesson.

If this were a musical

I'd shore myself up by the last act, singing at the top of my voice, some version of *what doesn't kill you only makes you stronger!* Backed by a thousand-Beyoncé gospel choir. A defiant chant, an empowering affirmation: How I have always survived. With or without them. I had and can still make it on my own.

And if this were a rom-com

She and I would argue over the guest lists — me whittling the numbers down as she demanded each long-estranged neighbor and every once-met acquaintance to join in the celebration. She would make the case for buffet over plate settings, while lecturing Jake on tea ceremony etiquettes — which elders to serve first, and how to hand over the red packets for safekeeping after we received them. They'd change their mind, rushing through airplanes and airports, dashing in time to walk me down the aisle. Later, we would laugh and tease one another during our speeches — who was the bigger bridezilla? My mother or I? Then, the obligatory redeeming reveal: that she was indeed planning for the wedding she never had herself. We'd dance the night away, as orchestral music swells to the scrolling of end credits.

But this is real life.

Not some story. Populated by some made-up characters. Who stumbled upon epiphanies in the light of day, after a long communion with the dark night of the soul. Who knew how to make amends and hug tearfully. And all would be forgiven.

Instead, there was only *I'm sorry in advance.* Which really means, a knowing regret. So why do it? Why not attempt the right thing in the first place when you can? Perhaps in their version of this story: I am the unfilial son whose joy is selfish and profane. Insufferable.

And no matter how I start this, the ending's the same: The presence of their absence, filling pages.

auto-correct

stop

        countries and colors do not need capitalization. or the very first letter of
the first word to every sentence. i am not a race: the weight of the punch
lie at the end at times and i am not more important than she or he or they
or it, or you.

so, no

        thanks to your suggestions (or are they admonitions?). red squiggly lines,
double-underlined blue flags colonizing the pristine of my page. you kill
what i'm yet to birth. new worlds through new words are not meant to fit
easily to your rightrigidrules.

for you

        are not correct by default and i'm not *wrongwrongwrong*.

LSOL: Love for Speakers of Other Languages

My first language is Fear — an amulet forged in scarcity warding off the misfortune of political instability and tragedy of financial insecurity.

My mother tongue is Shame — I speak it fluently in my dreams of victims and victors, competitors and conquerors, the hunted and the hunters.

Its dialects are Regret and Resentment — like rings of coffee stains on corners of pages I can't erase.

So when you talk to me about Love, it's a foreign film I've heard of before of course. Whose poster hung on my wall and trailer I've watched on repeat. But tickets I simply can't afford.

Teach me and I will learn to elongate every *uh-* and every *ah-*. I promise to practice and enunciate with no trace of an accent.

Speak it to me: I might just make it home.

Chlorine Chronicles

When I smell that smell — I am there again. Throat dry arms raised knees bent butt clenched privates tucked snug in the slinky safety of my speedo. The nakedness of my teenage body for all to see. Feet at the edge of the platform — alert poised ready. The horn blares, and I leap.

When I smell that — my father's head bobs up and down in and out on the other edge of the pool. We come here almost every morning in the summer. It's the only activity we do together. Yet he is in his lane, and I'm in mine, next to him. I paddle fast and reach the end — before him, and not because he is letting me this time.

When I — am one of the boys again stripping under the showers amidst the echoing chatter and chuckles: *who's the better kisser and which girl gives the best head?* I turn and he looks at me looking at him. I don't turn away, I can't look away. He is only a year older but taller than all of us; holding court, proud. Hair clinging all around his thighs. Inviting me taunting me to look at him taking him all in. Drinking my fill.

When — the rhythmic splish-splash, one breath over another as I kick as I pull as I glide between weight and weightlessness. A part of and apart from the water. I am wrapped in her embrace every square inch, every crevice. Once again washed clean.

The Way Back

For months, after you suddenly disappeared from your room, they said, "She will be home soon" — muttered like a prayer, as though saying and hearing it often enough, it would become true.

Later, as we camped out at the funeral hall — Pa, Ma, Ci, and I — in front of the elaborate altar where monks and nuns chanted their prayers in circles, the same adults would comfort us kids with, "Your grandmother is in a better place now." Dressed in all-white, we bowed as the next group of relatives lit their joss sticks and placed them in a metal bowl. Sandalwood smoke grew thick in the air as cardboard boxes of uneaten dinner laid strewn across the table. On the floor sat small hills of cracked-open peanut shells and half-empty disposable plastic cups of mineral water.

The morning before we laid you to rest, Pa asked whether I wanted to pay my last respects. I nodded and he led me to you, staring back from the framed black-and-white photo atop your casket. You always had that scowl on your face when you were alive. Perhaps they were right: *You're in a much better place now.*

Climbing up to the front of the van, squeezed in between Pa and the driver, I clung onto that image of you that was entrusted to me. We snailed across town to the burial ground in bumper-to-bumper traffic as Pa instructed me to call out turn-by-turn the route we were on. When pressed for a reason, he explained that this was our custom, that this was how you'd make your way back home. Under my breath, I whispered while you rested snugly on my lap: *Amah, we're crossing the train tracks now… then left at the intersection… followed by a right after this bridge…* Heavy rain washed the windowpane gray.

It was only when Pa shook me awake that I realized I had been asleep for some time. I dragged my feet under Ma's umbrella, rubbing my eyes, groggy and guilty. Pa scattered white flower petals as the groundskeepers lowered you into that muddy hole in the field. I caught everyone by surprise when I finally bawled then — an unstoppable series of sobs that pierced through the rain-blurred hill. I thought I had let you down. I thought you'd never find your way back again.

On our return, I sat in front of the same van, lodged once more in between Pa and the driver, staying up and alert this time, speaking aloud, *Turn left after the bridge, right at the intersection, then pass the train tracks…* until I had them memorized by heart.

It was years later when I came to learn that those directions home weren't for you. They were for me.

A Feast for Amah

i

Thick congealed slab of yellow margarine then a rainfall of coarse-grain sugar on plain white bread. He didn't know they had no jam or butter in the cool box. He didn't know this was luxury for her, squatting down in shelters, air raids thunderous above. To this day he still asks for packets from flight attendants furrowing at him funny before their carts of coffee and tea roll down the aisles. When the plane dips she holds his hands steady as he pries into half the dinner roll from corners of tinfoil trays slathering and sprinkling, biting off a piece of that salt and sweet sinking soft in his belly.

ii

By the early morning light, she hauls that sack of sweet potatoes off our kitchen floor stocked seemingly just for this occasion. Peeling and dicing them into cubes before washing a cup of jasmine rice in the sink three times as she'd taught you once before. One to clean, two for taste, and three for luck. Then boiling them into gooey mush. No doubt your fever will break and cough dissipate as she nurses into you that spoonful of porridge streaked orange from sinewy fibrous roots. We come from a long line of peasant farmers after all — her hands alchemize comfort out of crumbs, and sustenance from scraps. Sick days are your favorite.

Long sweaty dusty walks back from school are tolerable knowing I'll sink your teeth into those juicy treats she's prepared. Every day, without fail, a bowl of ripe oranges sliced into quarters de-seeded and chilled in the fridge, waiting for me. Over and over again, I'll chase after this pulpy parade of ice-cold fireworks in my mouth — a chance to sketch once more the ghostly scent of citrus sunbeams exploding in the air.

Multi-Color Self-Care

Caring for myself is not self-indulgence,
it is self-preservation, and that is an act of political warfare.
— Audre Lorde

When the world turns bleak and blue, and words are rainstorms I drown in — I open my drawer and pick up those gold for the rustling leaves in the breeze, red for the yawning sun ready to be cradled by Night's sleep, and green for spring waiting in the wings to bloom.

Cracked Vase

After a sweaty day meandering through rows and rows of stalls perusing the second-hand items on sale, I stopped for a rest in front of an antique shop in my hometown Jakarta.

Like others on the street, this was no fancy establishment. No gold-plated gleaming mirrors or hundred-year-old teak wood cabinets with intricate carvings within the paint-flaking walls. The graveyard of discarded junk on the outdoor display table — a pitiful parade of boxy television sets, dial-up modems from the previous millennium, and keyboards with missing buttons — only stoked my increasing irritability of not finding what I was looking for, since I didn't know what I was looking for in the first place.

Amidst the monochromatic gray and black sea of bric-a-brac, a lone vase buoyed to the surface — its crimson-red glaze shimmering in the late afternoon sun. I held my breath as I inched my way toward it for a closer look.

Lopsided and lumpy, its surface was rough and irregular as though the potter had finished in a hurry, not bothering to sand it down. It might have even fallen and crashed more than once. Water would probably leak through the jagged spiderwebs of dark copper lacquer barely holding this makeshift kintsugi together. Holding the clay container in one hand, its solid weight settling into my grasp, I traced with my finger the sharp, chipped rim — the ghostly indentation of a snaggletooth.

It was at that moment I heard a familiar laugh.

Was that…? But it couldn't possibly be. There was no one around. Besides, she had been dead for 25 years now if that was who I thought I'd just heard.

Turning my attention back to the vase, I gasped — finding in its reflection the face of my amah: my father's mother, the loose change-scrounger and plastic bag-hoarder who lived through one colonial occupation, one foreign invasion, one independence revolution, and one military coup that exploded into a full-blown massacre. Her pockmarked face, and the weathered wrinkles around her mouth and crow's feet by her eyes pulled tight.

Brutally broken and still beautiful, she was beaming.

Sign Post

> *I gave the skin to my love and said, Now I am a story—*
> *like the snake, I am my own future.*
> — Natalie Diaz

We are snakes

    and the stories we tell are skins

Peel them — off our backs

    shed them when they get too tight

        and hang them on trees

            so they *scale with light*

      to catch the eyes

    of those who will come after

                to continue the fight

ENDNOTES

Several pieces in this collection refer to the tumultuous period from 1965 to 2000 when the Indonesian government instituted a series of forced assimilation laws that directly discriminated against the minority Indonesian Chinese community in the country: barring Chinese language names on official documents, banning Chinese language media and schools, as well as prohibiting public celebrations of cultural festivals such as Chinese New Year.

These discriminatory policies stoked the general populace's resentment and prejudices toward the community that led to lootings and arsons of homes and businesses, sexual assaults, and massacres of Indonesian Chinese in 1965 and again in 1998.

"The Question Next Time" — The title echoes James Baldwin's *The Fire Next Time*.

"Love Refugees" — The term "refugee" is not a metaphor in this piece. Faced with real fear of persecution and the threat of violence due to the discriminatory policies instituted by the government, countless Indonesian Chinese families have fled the country through documented and undocumented channels from the 1960s to 2000s.

"LSOL: Love for Speakers of Other Languages" — The title echoes "ESOL: English for Speakers of Other Languages" programs.

"Cracked Vase" — A Dutch colony for over 200 years, Indonesia was occupied by the Japanese during WWII. After the country gained independence in 1949, a violent military coup erupted into a massacre where thousands of Indonesian Chinese and suspected Communists were killed or simply "disappeared."

"Cognitive Reframing" — This piece is inspired by and written as an homage to "ars pasifika" by Craig Santos Perez.

"Multi-Color Self-Care" — The epigraph is from Audre Lorde.

"Sign Post" — The epigraph and phrase "scale with light" are from Natalie Diaz's poem "Snake-Light."

ACKNOWLEDGMENTS

My immense gratitude goes to:

… the Foglifter team: Luiza Flynn-Goodlett, Miah Jeffra, Jason Lipeles, Chad Koch, and Susan Calvillo; Start a Riot! jury panel: Gabriele Christian, Chekwube Danladi, and Reid Gomez; RADAR Productions; and Still Here San Francisco for believing in this collection.

… these publications and organizations for their generous support:
- *The Ana*: "Love Refugees," "LSOL: Love for Speakers of Other Languages," and "Sign Post"
- *Beyond Queer Words* anthology: "The Question Next Time"
- *The Gay and Lesbian Review*: "The Man on the Train"
- Browning Society, Leonard Isaacson Award: "The Way Back"
- GAPA Theatre: "A Feast for Amah"
- Story Center: "Cracked Vase"
- Take Place x *The Ana*: "A Feast for Amah," "Cracked Vase," and "The Way Back"
- San Francisco State University, Poetry Center (New Voice): "Dear Future Ex," "Chlorine Chronicles," and "tap tap tap."

… my creative comrades: Josh Kim and Tracy Gross-Kahn; and the Gunawan-Lucchi family: Pa, Ma, Ci, Dek, Lori, Chris, Tessa, Daniel, Carly, and Jen. A special shout-out goes to SFSU Poetry Center and London Pinkney, Carlos Quinteros III, and TreVaughn Roach-Carter at *The Ana* for being first in recognizing and affirming my voice.

… the larger literary and artistic community for much-appreciated guidance and encouragement: May-lee Chai, Carolina de Robertis, Andrew Joron, Matthew Clark Davison, Nona Caspers, Sophie Clavier, Lily Kaylor Honoré, Samantha Cosentino, and May-Li Khoe at San Francisco State University's MFA in Creative Writing program; Xu Xi and Ira Sukrungruang at Authors at Large; Gregg Schroeder and Marshall Moore at Tong Zhi Literary Group; Leva Zand at ARTogether; Jason Bayani, Mihee Kim, and Michelle Lin at Kearny Street Workshop; César Cadabes, Joel Tan, and Kat Evasco at GAPA Theatre; Amy Hill at Story Center; John Nguyen, Alder Duan Hurley, Angeera Khadka, Viola Lasmana, Margaret Rhee, Paula Te, Scott Lankford, Julie Bruck, and S. Brook Corfman; and everyone who'd taken the time and care to read and provide feedback on my work — *thankyouthankyouthankyou*.

… and dearest Jake and Exxo — for being Home.

ELBERT LIM, ILLUSTRATOR

Elbert Lim is an Indonesian visual storyteller.

In 2019, he founded Khayalan Arts — a creative studio that works on socially-impactful art projects, video games, installations, exhibitions, webcomics, workshops, and beach cleanup activities.

He is also the creator and head developer of the multi award-winning *SAMUDRA*, an atmospheric video game that addresses the global threat of ocean pollution. A recipient of the Unity for Humanity Grant & Microsoft Diverse Creative Funds, the project launched in September 2021 on Steam, and is porting for console release in 2022. For more, visit khayalanarts.com.

EDWARD GUNAWAN, POET

Edward Gunawan is a writer and filmmaker.

The creator of *The Life Cycle of Water* — a collection of non-fiction video essays and cine-poems (a recipient of the East Bay Fund for Artists and City of Oakland's Neighborhood Voices Artist grants), he is also the writer of *Press Play* — an award-winning non-fiction webcomic that has been translated into six languages and published as a chapbook by Sweet Lit. His work has also been published in *TriQuarterly, Aquifer: Florida Review Online,* and *The Gay & Lesbian Review.*

As writer, producer, actor, and/or director, he has completed over 25 feature films and shorts that were screened at Berlin, Locarno, and Cadence film festivals. With support from the Marcus Recruitment Award and Edward B. Kaufmann's Scholarship, he is completing his MFA in Creative Writing at San Francisco State University.

A queer Indonesian-born Chinese immigrant, Edward now lives with his husband and their dog on unceded Ohlone land in Oakland, CA. For more, visit addword.com.

Rooted in the San Francisco Bay Area, Foglifter Press is a platform for LGBTQ+ writers that supports and uplifts powerful, intersectional, and transgressive queer and trans writing through publication and public readings to build and enrich our communities as well as the greater literary arts.

Eye the margins.

www.foglifterpress.com